# Naya's Little Lionheart

## Crystal Nicholson

First published in 2021

Written by Crystal Nicholson
Illustrated by Coraline Tran
Interior page design Bryony van der Merwe

ISBN: 978-1-7359296-0-6 (paperback)
ISBN: 978-1-7359296-1-3 (hardcover)

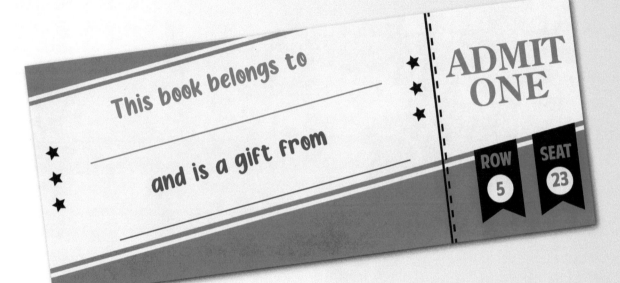

This book belongs to

and is a gift from

ADMIT ONE

ROW 5

SEAT 23

Naya felt the warmth of the spotlight on her face.

She squinted to see her teacher, Mr. Pie, beyond the bright lights of the school stage as she heard his voice loudly boom:

"YOU MAY BEGIN, NAYA!"

Naya's hands were so sweaty that she thought the microphone would slip from her fingers. She took a deep breath and sang the song she chose for the school musical audition.

"Today is –"

Her voice squeaked and cracked.
She cleared her throat and tried again,
"Today—"

The next time she opened her mouth, her voice barely let out a sound.

There was a **squeak so tiny** that she sounded like a mouse. Her stomach felt sick. She dropped the microphone and threw her hands to her face.

tears burned her cheeks as they rolled past her chin.

Mr. Pie **rushed** over to her.

"It's okay, Naya," he said, kneeling. "There will be another audition in a few days. Practice, and then you can audition again."

Naya wiped the tears from her face and left the stage.

Exit

It seemed to take forever to reach the exit doors but as she did, she heard a **beautiful ballad** echo throughout the building.

"Today is the day that I will take what's mine! Today is the day that I will sparkle and shine!"

Naya whipped around to see where the singing was coming from. Her mouth dropped open as she realized it was the new student, Rosie, auditioning.

Rosie had just moved to Naya's street recently, so Naya knew nothing about her. She especially didn't know that she was such **an incredible singer!**

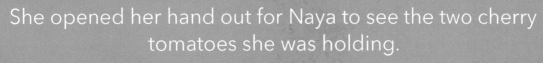

She opened her hand out for Naya to see the two cherry tomatoes she was holding.

"See how these tomatoes are different sizes and unique shades of red?" she asked.

"They both look beautiful, though, right?"

Naya nodded.

They both need the sunshine to become the best little tomatoes they can be, but they share it! Just focus on *growing your talent* while knowing that sharing the sunshine with Rosie won't stop you from becoming the best version of yourself.

Naya ate one of the delicious tomatoes
from Mama's hand and
**thought deeply**
about what she said.

Sparkle and shine!

Naya spent the
next two days practicing non-stop.
She sang for her stuffies: Mr. Bear,
Lolly the Lamb, Starlight the Fox,
and Zoey the Zebra.

She sang in the bathtub.

She sang for her dog.

She even sang in her dreams!

ENCORE! ENCORE!

While Naya was outside singing to the birds, she saw Rosie riding her bike nearby. She remembered what her mother had said to her in the garden.

# It's time to share the sunshine,

she thought.

**"HEY, ROSIE!"**

Naya shouted from across the lawn. "Do you want to practice for the audition together?"

"Yes, sure!" Rosie said as she put her bike down in the grass.
"I saw your audition the other day. Did you have stage fright?" she asked.

"What's that?" Naya asked.

"It's when you're nervous about performing in front of people. Some people get scared stiff!" she said as she stiffened her body like a board.

Naya threw her head back and giggled. "Yes, I guess I did have stage fright.

Do you have it, too?" she asked.

"No, but that's because I have this," Rosie said, showing Naya a beautiful necklace with a lion charm on it. "My friend at my old school gave this to me to wear so I can remember to be like this lion- fearless and strong."

"It's pretty," Naya said.

Rosie looked at her and smiled. She took the necklace off and held it out as an offering for Naya.

"It's yours now," Rosie said, eyes sparkling. "When you're on stage, just remember that you don't need to be scared because you have the heart of a brave lion!"

"Wow, thank you!"

Naya exclaimed. "It's the best gift anyone has ever given me!"

Naya and Rosie sang together every day. Naya felt confident and free while practicing with her new best friend, but she was so nervous on the big day that her stomach felt as if there were **butterflies fluttering inside of it.**

Rosie turned to her.
"Remember, your lion is with
you. Be fearless! Be brave!
I'll see you after your
audition."

Naya took a deep breath and stood on stage with her little lionheart beat racing. She got nervous when the spotlight shined on her, but she was ready to show the class how much she had grown.

Today is the day that I will take what's mine!
Today is the day that I will sparkle and shine!"

Her voice didn't crack or squeak! She moved across the stage, dancing to the beat while she continued her song.

"I can do whatever I set my mind to, and I'm going to make my dreams come true!"

Later that day, Naya roared through the house and into the kitchen where her family gathered.

"I got a part in the musical!"

she shrieked in excitement. "It's the second biggest part of the show!"

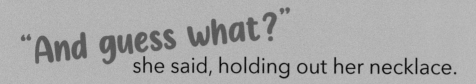

## "And guess what?"

she said, holding out her necklace.

"The necklace that Rosie gave me helped me feel brave onstage. I was nervous, but I remembered this little lion."

"Oh, Naya! That's so wonderful!" Mama cooed.
"You must be so proud of yourself, little lionheart!"
she said as she snuggled her face into Naya's.

This was, by far, Naya's favorite part of this
**whole magical day.**

# ABOUT THE AUTHOR

Crystal Nicholson dreamed of being a writer from as far back as she can remember. Although it took some time to finally write and publish her first book, *Naya's Little Lionheart*, Crystal has many more books to write and stories to share.

The central themes of her books will be self-love, confidence and friendship. These are also the lessons the very proud grandmother intends to instill in her lovely granddaughter, Rosie.

Crystal hopes that Rosie will grow up in a diverse and inclusive world that champions differences and recognizes that people have more in common than they initially believe.

When not writing or partaking in her favorite hobbies, she enjoys her life with her wife, Lesli, and their four pets in the beautiful forest of Northern California where they reside.

CPSIA information can be obtained
at www.ICGtesting.com
Printed in the USA
BVHW020344011021
617787BV00003B/68